Making
new friends

Grolier Enterprises Inc. offers a varied selection of both
adult and children's book racks. For details on ordering,
please write: Grolier Enterprises Inc., Sherman Turnpike,
Danbury, CT 06816 Attn: Premium Department

Published in the United States by Grolier Enterprises, Inc.
Danbury, Connecticut 06816.

Originally published in the United States by
Modern Promotions/Publishers, a Division of Unisystems, Inc.

Designed by Victoria House Publishing Limited, Paulton, Bristol BS18 5LQ

Jane Carruth   illustrated by Tony Hutchings

Making new friends

GROLIER ENTERPRISES INC.
Danbury, Connecticut 06816
Printed in Yugoslavia

Chippy was a rather timid squirrel. When all the
other little squirrels were out playing in the forest,
he was too shy to join in. He liked to play at home,
with his Mommy.
One day a letter arrived. "Oh, dear," said Mommy.
"Grandma is not well. I must go to see her."

"Come along, Chippy," said Mommy. "Mrs. Nutmeg
will look after you today, and you will have a lot
of fun with the family."
"I'd rather stay at home with you," cried Chippy.

The Nutmeg family all gave Chippy a warm welcome
when he arrived. "Hello, will you come and play
with us?" they smiled.
But Chippy felt very upset. He didn't even say
goodbye to his mother as she went away.

They all had lunch, with good things to eat.

Chippy didn't feel hungry. He looked at a book.

After lunch the little squirrels ran outside to play
with their ball. Chippy was still feeling shy. He sat
down with his book.
"Why don't you join in the game?" asked Susie
Nutmeg. "There are only three of us, but if you play
as well, we can make two teams."

"No, I don't want to play," said Chippy. He took no notice of the game, but suddenly the ball bounced right into his lap, and knocked the book to one side.

"Quick, throw it back!" called Susie.

Chippy couldn't help joining in the game after that. The squirrels raced through the branches, throwing the ball to each other. Soon they were near the goal, a hole in the tree trunk.

Chippy was just in the right place to catch the ball,
and quickly he turned around and tossed it straight
into the goal.
"Hooray! We've won!" cried Susie happily.
"Well done, Chippy!" said the others.

After the game they had milk and cookies. "You
played very well," said the little squirrels to
Chippy. "It was a terrific game!"
"Yes, I really enjoyed it," laughed Chippy. He had
forgotten to be shy.
When Chippy's mother came back, she was
surprised to see the party.

Chippy was having such fun that he hardly noticed his mother coming to get him. "They have all had a lovely day," said Mrs. Nutmeg.
Mommy was glad to see Chippy playing with the others. But it was time to go home. "I wish I could stay!" cried Chippy.

The Nutmegs waved goodbye to Chippy. "Take the ball and practice at home," they called. "Come and have another game with us soon!" "Thanks, I certainly shall," smiled Chippy, as they set off home.